4

CROWN OF LOVE

STORY & ART BY YUN KOUGA

Table of Contents

Story Thus Far

When Hisayoshi helps Rima get into Hakuô High, the two grow closer, but it doesn't last. Hisayoshi is irritated by his unreciprocated love, and Rima begins to distance herself from him. When Rima utterly rejects him one morning, Hisayoshi starts avoiding her. Then Rima's old crush Ikeshiba kisses her, and she comes to the realization that she no longer has feelings for him...

Rima Fujio

Hisayoshi "Kumi" Tajima

Shingo Tachibana

Ikeshiba

CROWN
OF LOVE

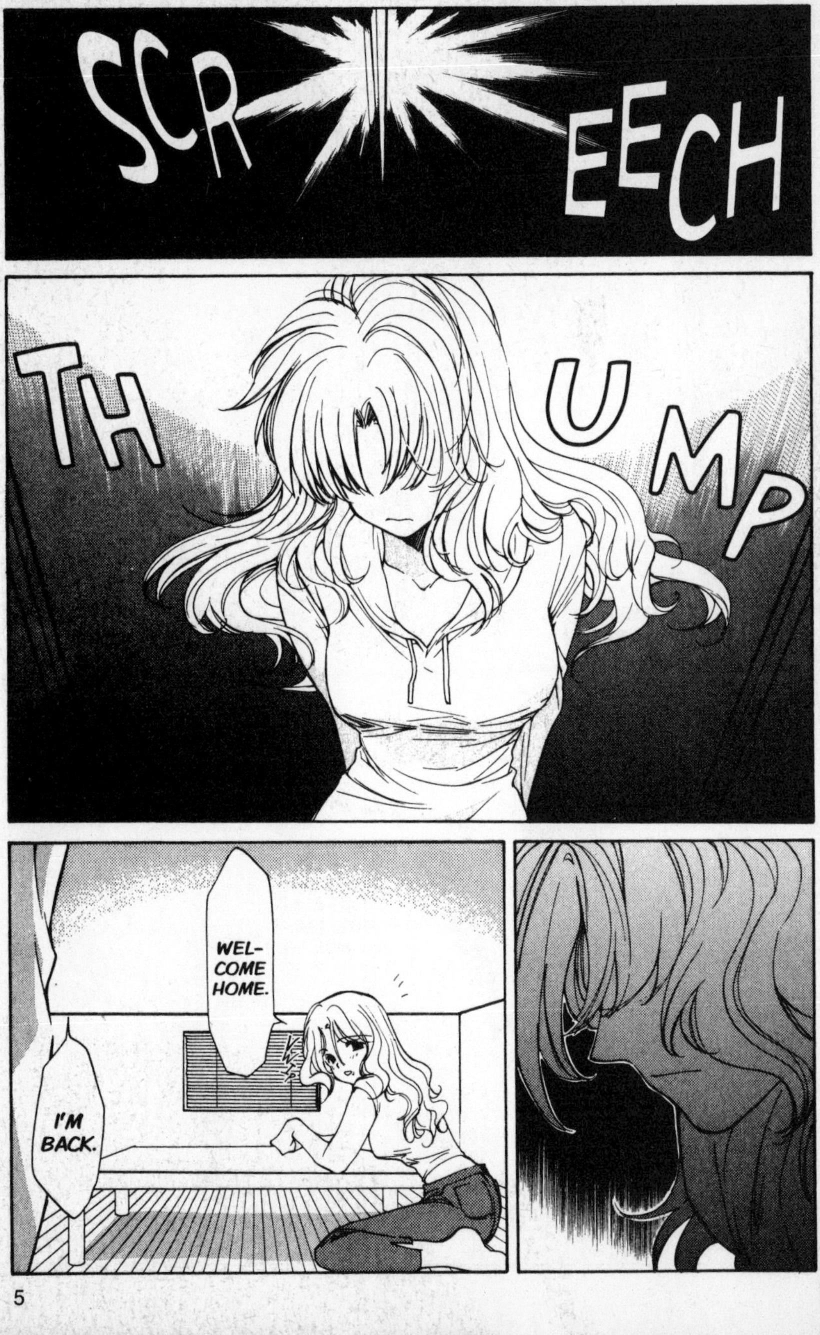

TH
UMP

TMP
RIMA?
?
NOK
WHAT'S WRONG? DID SOMETHING HAPPEN?
SOMETHING?
WHAT DO YOU MEAN BY SOMETHING?
ARGH!
Yikes! Scary!
WHY ARE YOU SO COLD TO YOUR MOTHER?
SCREEECH
IT'S NOTHING. GO AWAY.
HEEHEE
I'M SO SORRY, MUMMY DEAREST.
I'm really scared!

KUMI-CHAN, YOUR PHONE'S RINGING.

DOODEE DOODOO DEE

JUST LEAVE IT.

I DON'T WANT TO ANSWER IT.

DOOP DEE DOO
WHO IS IT?
IT SAYS "FUJIO, HOME."
FLINCH

DOOP
OH HEY, IT'S RIMA.
DEE DOO
THAT'S OKAY.
I DON'T WANT TO ANSWER.

HISAYOSHI! THAT'S NOT RIGHT!
THUNK
I DON'T WANNA.
HUH?
DOOP DEE DOO

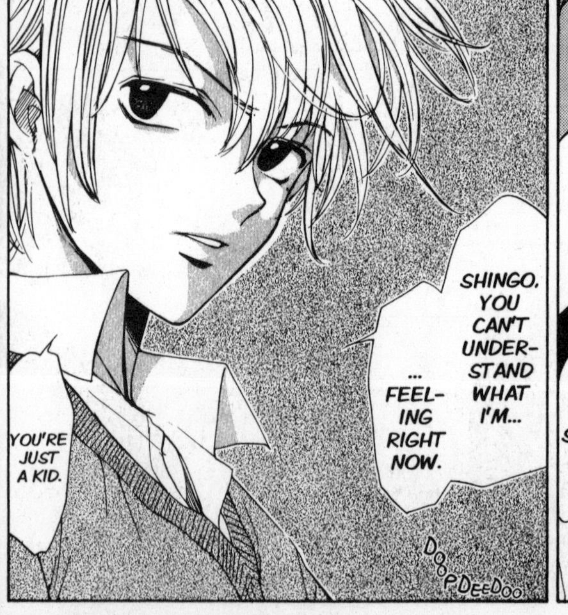

SHINGO, YOU CAN'T UNDERSTAND WHAT I'M...
... FEELING RIGHT NOW.
YOU'RE JUST A KID.
DOOP DEE DOO

DOOP DEEDOO
DOOP DEEDOO
KUMI-CHAN...
URGH
H-HOW COULD I KNOW?!
YOU'RE BEING REALLY RUDE!
IF YOU DON'T CUT IT OUT, I'M GOING TO GET REALLY FED UP WITH YOU!
HOW WOULD I KNOW HOW YOU FEEL?!
DOOP-DEE DOO
HOW WOULD I KNOW HOW IT FEELS TO BE...
...TALL AND GOOD-LOOKING...
...AND THE SAME AGE AS RIMA?!
DOOP DEE DOO
NOTHING I HAVE IS GOOD ENOUGH!

KLLIK

OOH.

AT LEAST TALK TO HER.

I'M LOSING PATIENCE WITH YOU.

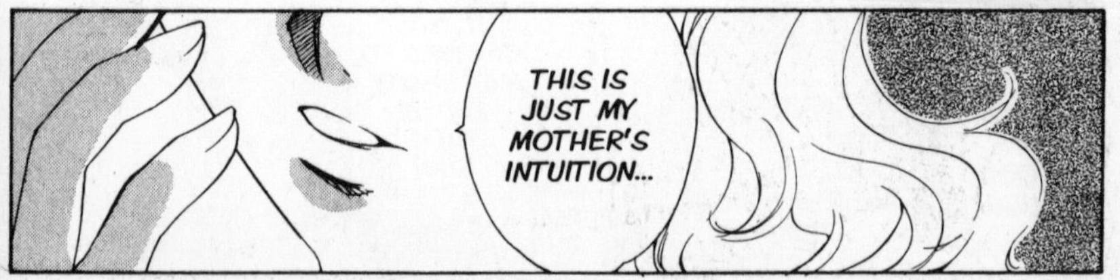
THIS IS JUST MY MOTHER'S INTUITION...

WEAK ENING
OH GREAT.
MITSUKO-SAN?
THAT'S A NICE GREETING.
ARE YOU DISAPPOINTED IT'S NOT RIMA?
NOT REALLY.

SOMETHING HAPPENED BETWEEN YOU TWO, RIGHT?
SHE'S ACTING REALLY WEIRD.

SULK

HEY, KUMI-CHAN, WHAT HAPPENED?!
ARE YOU LISTENING?
NO, I'M NOT.
WHAT?!

YOU BETTER COME TO THE HOUSE RIGHT NOW.

I'VE GOT NO CHOICE THEN. I'M COMING TO SEE YOU.

NO! YOU'D JUST BE A NUISANCE!

YOU—

WHY WOULD I GO AT THIS HOUR?

THIS IS IKESHIBA-SAN'S HOUSE.

COME TO THE HOUSE.

NO.

I SAID NO!

WHAT, THEN?

SHF

KUMI-CHAN?

SHF

I'M GOING OUT.

IT'S AFTER NINE!

I'LL BE BACK BEFORE THE TRAINS STOP RUNNING.

KUMI-CHAN.

Dammit...

Night.

I rush out of the house...

...after a woman calls me.

IF...
...it...
...had been Rima on the phone...
KLIK
I'M HOME!
WEL-COME HOME.
NICE TO SEE YOU.
GOOD EVE-NING.

HUH.
WHERE'S HISA-YOSHI-KUN?

SILENCE

HELLO?
...

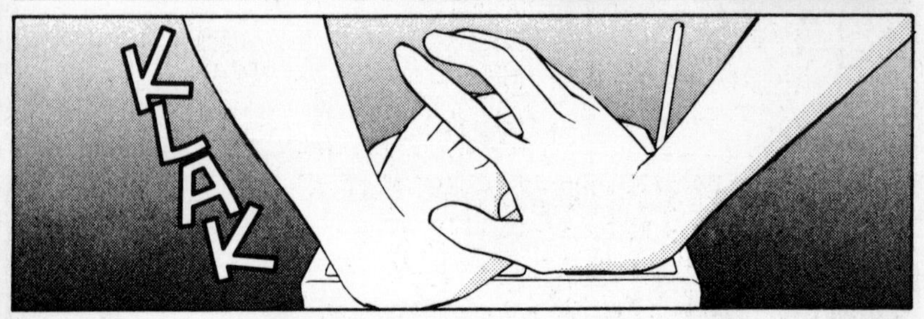
KLAK

SKRICH
RIMA?
I'M GOING OUT FOR A BIT.

AT LEAST ANSWER ME.
LOCK YOUR DOOR AND GO TO SLEEP, OKAY?
SILENCE
...
SIGH
RING
DAD, PHONE ...
IT'S RIMA-CHAN.
HMM.

ORIHI

NEW MENU

KLAK

OVER HERE, KUMI-CHAN!

WHAT'RE YOU SO ANGRY ABOUT?

I'M NOT.

I WON'T LET YOU GO HOME UNTIL YOU SPILL.
TU NK
WHAT'S WRONG WITH RIMA?

MITSUKO-SAN, YOU SHOULDN'T BUTT IN SO MUCH.
WHY NOT? I'M HER MOTHER.
IF THINGS GO WELL, I MAY EVEN BE YOUR MOTHER SOMEDAY, HISAYOSHI-KUN.
DON'T BE STUPID.
SO DID YOU DO IT?

KLUNK
WHA-?!
HEY!
DO WHAT?
WHAT DO YOU THINK?

That night...

PLEASE DON'T SEXUALLY HARASS ME LIKE THAT.
IT MAKES ME FEEL GUILTY.

...was really messed up.

HOW RUDE! THIS ISN'T HARASSMENT.
IT'S A MOTHER'S, OR SHOULD I SAY, A WOMAN'S INTUITION.
WHY DOES IT MAKE YOU FEEL GUILTY?
SULK

It was him.

I had no proof.

I'M GOING HOME.
DIZZY
HUH?
W-WAIT, HISA-YOSHI-KUN!
I won't let you go!
KLAK
He did something to her!
Why?
Why?
Why?!

IKE-SHIBA!
WAKE UP, ASS-HOLE!
JOLT
WHAT THE...?
WHAT'RE YOU DOING, HISA-YOSHI-KUN?
You startled me.
IT'S THE MIDDLE OF THE NIGHT.
SHUT UP! KEEP IT DOWN.
YOU'LL WAKE MANAMI.
GRRR
HUFF HUFF
...
I'M GOING TO COME STRAIGHT OUT WITH IT.
GRR
GRR GRR
GRR
YOU DID SOME-THING TO RIMA AGAIN, DIDN'T YOU?
I DON'T KNOW WHAT YOU'RE TALKING ABOUT!
LET'S TALK IN THE MORN-ING.
NO! DON'T PLAY DUMB!
GRAB
GASP

I'M BEG- GING YOU.
IF YOU DON'T ...
...I'LL NEVER FALL ASLEEP.
BUT I...
... DON'T KNOW.
URGH!
YAWN
I DIDN'T DO ANY- THING.
YOU'RE TAKING ADVANTAGE OF HOW NICE I ALWAYS AM.
TELL ME!
THE TRUTH!
I AM. I DON'T KNOW. I DIDN'T DO ANY- THING.
GOOD NIGHT!
IKE- SHIBA!

PLEASE!
PLEASE TELL ME THE TRUTH.
OKAY.
DID YOU DO SOMETHING TO RIMA?
I'LL BELIEVE YOU.
What a wonderful guy you are.
I'LL TELL YOU THE TRUTH.
I'M TELLING YOU, I DIDN'T DO ANY-THING.

...
REALLY ?
I BELIEVE YOU.
YEAH.
BELIEVE ME.
It's a harsh world.
... ...
...
SORRY ABOUT THAT.
MMM-HMM.
NIGHT!
IF you think I can't lie to you when you look me right in the eyes...
...then you really are just a kid.

If you think adults are always nice to children...

...you're making a big mistake.

TWEET

Good morning!

This is the seven o'clock news!

KLINK

DAD, WILL YOU BE EATING AT HOME TONIGHT?

SHF

I'LL GIVE YOU A CALL.

...
KUMI-CHAN'S LATE.
MM...
HE'S GOING TO BE LATE FOR...
HE WAS SNEAKING AROUND LATE LAST NIGHT.
KLIK
IS HE STILL SULKING?
SIP

I'm running away.
Please don't worry
about me.
DAD!
KUMI-CHAN RAN AWAY.
DAD!
HE'S GONE!
FLAP
HE LEFT A NOTE!
HUH?

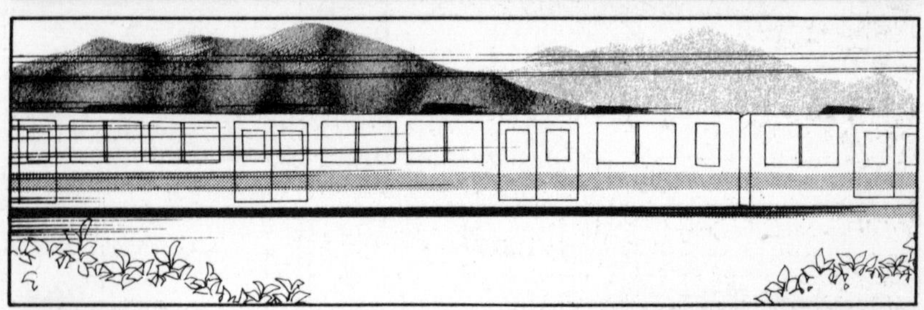

I'm running away.
Please don't worry
about me.

THIS IS WHAT HE DOES THE SECOND HE HAS A PROBLEM.
KUMI-CHAN LIKES RUNNING AWAY.
MAYBE IT'S A HABIT?

What should I tell Hisa-kuni-san?
Hisayoshi's Dad
Hmm...
What should I tell Shingo-kun?
I think he'll be worried.

KLATA
KLATA
KLATA

Oh god...
The first inbound train is really crowded.
KA-THUNK
The out-bound is empty.
KA-THUNK

FAREWELL, SALARYMEN!
I'M HEADING OUTBOUND.
KA-THUNK
I AM...
... RUNNING AWAY.
KA-THUNK

KA-THUNK
KA-THUNK
KA-THUNK

SPLISH

WHAT?! HISA-YOSHI DID?!
HISAYOSHI REALLY LOVES RUNNING AWAY FROM HOME!
OH, PUT SOME RUM IN THAT.
ABOUT TWO DROPS.
Orange juice.
NO, SHINGO-SAMA.

POOR THING. I WONDER WHERE HE WENT?
HE WENT OFF ALL ALONE WITHOUT EVEN TELLING ME, HIS BFF.
I'LL LET YOU KNOW IF I HEAR FROM HIM.

SHINGO-KUN DOESN'T KNOW EITHER.
...
DO YOU AND... SHINGO-KUN... TALK ON THE PHONE A LOT?
HUH? YEAH.
WE EMAIL TOO.
HMM ...

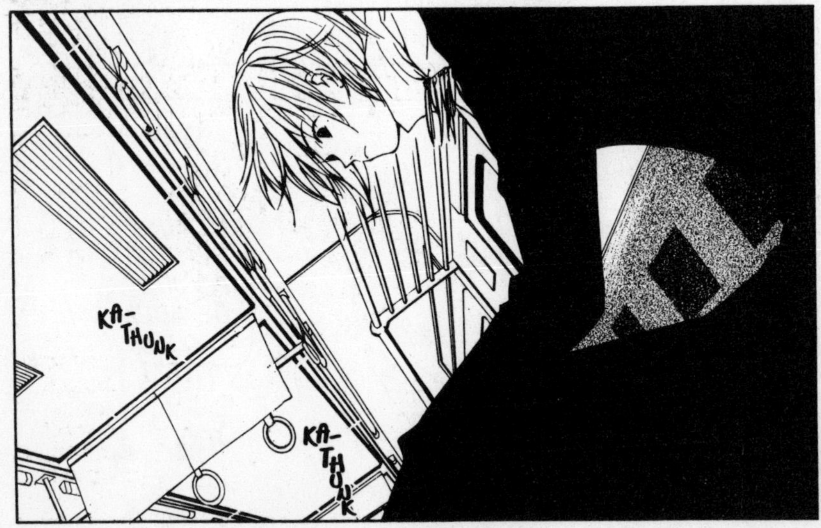
KA-THUNK
KA-THUNK

TA-JIMA-KUN...
SULK
...LEFT?
THAT'S RIGHT. RIMA-CHAN, DO YOU HAVE ANY IDEA WHERE HE WENT?
NOT AT ALL.
OH.
RUN-NING AWAY...
STAB
IT MUST BE NICE TO JUST BE ABLE TO DO THAT!
STAB
STAB
OH YEAH?
She's pissed.
ARE YOU JEALOUS?

WHAT?!

Ack, she's really scary!

I'M SORRY.

THAT WAS A STUPID THING TO SAY.

BUT YOU KNOW ...

YOU LOOK A LITTLE TIRED TOO, RIMA-CHAN.

I'M POPULAR NOW.

I HAVE TO MAKE THE MOST OF IT WHILE I'M GETTING WORK.

YEESH.

THIS IS COMING FROM A 16-YEAR-OLD?

WELL, IT DOESN'T MATTER.
THINGS ARE MUCH MORE PEACEFUL WITH TAJIMA-KUN GONE.
SHEESH.

Rima-chan, please go in the booth now!

Okay!

Run away?
That's so irresponsible!

How immature! Tajima-kun is really such a baby!
Every-one's worried about him.

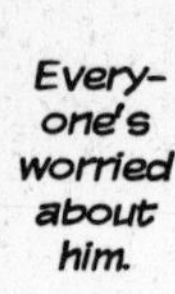
Except for me, of course.
Things are more peaceful with him gone.

...
...
HMM...
SQUEAK
...
...
SHE SEEMS... TO NOT BE CONCEN-TRATING.

HYOOO

SWIP

Somehow...

I ended up buying them.

They say eating one will add three years to your life.

But do I want... to live a longer life?

I'm starving.

I've lived 16 years without Rima...
I want to hurry up and start my life with Rima.
"So did you do it?"
BLUSH
IF...

...we had...
...I'd die.
I'd just die.
No, wait, dying would be a problem.
I mean, I couldn't die.
I don't care if I die.

BLUSH
Why am I thinking about not caring if I die...
...while I eat hard-boiled eggs?

HYOOO
Oh...
I'm sure Rima has no idea...
...that I want to do those things.
Sorry.

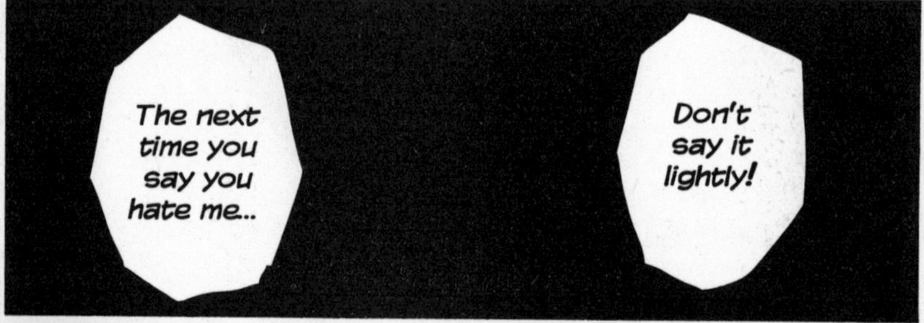
Don't say it lightly!
The next time you say you hate me...

JOLT
RIMA-CHAN?

VROOM
RIMA-CHAN, ARE YOU ALL RIGHT?
HARA-SAN.
SORRY, I MUST HAVE FALLEN ASLEEP.
OH?
...It looked like your eyes were open.
When I...
FSSH
...let my guard down, I...
WHAT WAS IT?
RIMA?
WHAT DO YOU CALL IT WHEN YOU REMEMBER SOMETHING...
NOT PONDERING...
A FLASHBACK?
Well, "pondering" is fine too though.
THAT'S IT.
BLUNT
GRIP
I'm remembering.

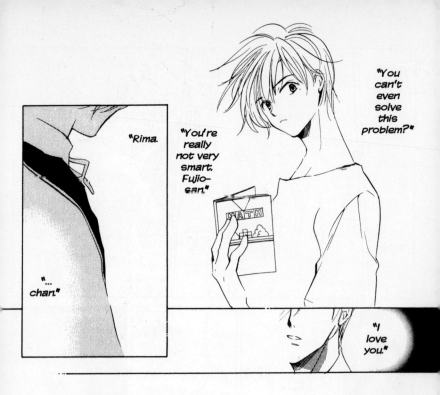

"You can't even solve this problem?"

"You're really not very smart, Fujio-san."

"Rima.

"... chan."

"I love you."

Why am I remembering all that?

HI ...
IT'S HISA-YOSHI.
I'M SORRY FOR DISAP-PEARING LIKE THAT.
YEAH.
I'M AT THE STATION NOW.
AT IZU.
I'M GOING TO STAY HERE TONIGHT.

MONEY?
I'VE GOT SOME... SORT OF.
SULK
I HAD THEM FIND ME A GUEST-HOUSE AT THE TOURIST INFORMATION BOOTH.
YEAH. LATER...
KLIK
PHEW...
GLOOMY
SIR. DINNER WILL BE SERVED AT SIX.
SIGH
THANKS.
YOU'VE STILL GOT SOME TIME. DID YOU WANT TO TAKE A BATH?
OR A WALK BY THE OCEAN MIGHT FEEL GOOD. IS THIS YOUR FIRST TIME AT A GUESTHOUSE?

YES. IT IS.
WE DON'T TEND TO OUR GUESTS MUCH AT A LODGE LIKE THIS ONE.
MEALS ARE SERVED IN THE COMMON ROOM, AND WE DON'T LAY OUT YOUR FUTON. YOU DO IT YOURSELF.

OKAY.
THAT'S WHY THE RATES ARE SO LOW.
BUT I'LL COME AND LAY OUT YOUR FUTON FOR YOU, SPECIAL.

NO. THAT'S OKAY.

Special!?

IT'S BEEN A WHILE SINCE WE'VE HAD SUCH A HANDSOME LAD AS YOU, SO I'M ALL FLUSTERED!

HA HA HA HA HA

HA HA HA HA

FWOOSH

FWOOSH

What am I doing calling and telling him where I am?

If I was going to regret it, I shouldn't have left in the first place.

But I didn't know I would until I did it.

When did I become such an idiot?

URGH...

If I'm going to regret things no matter what...

All I can do is what feels right at the time.

THAT'S ALL I CAN DO.
BUZZ
BUZZ
OH.
SO I HEARD FROM TOKUGAWA-KUN...
BUZZ
BUZZ
HMM?
DID HISAYOSHI-KUN REALLY RUN AWAY?
OH.

WELL, HE DID LEAVE A NOTE.
BUT I EXPECT HE'LL BE BACK SOON.
HE REALLY CAUSES SO MUCH TROUBLE!
I CAN'T FIGURE OUT IF HE'S AN ADULT OR A CHILD!
HMPH
NAH, 17-YEAR-OLD BOYS ARE LIKE BUGS...
HA HA
HA
... COMPARED TO GIRLS.
I HATE BUGS!
WELL, HE'S GOT A GOOD HEAD ON HIS SHOULDERS.
I'M SURE HE'S COMING BACK.
I'm actually...
...kind of shocked.
Even after what happened ...
I'm talking to Ikeshiba-san the same as usual.

I'm shocked that it didn't hurt me more.

Why?

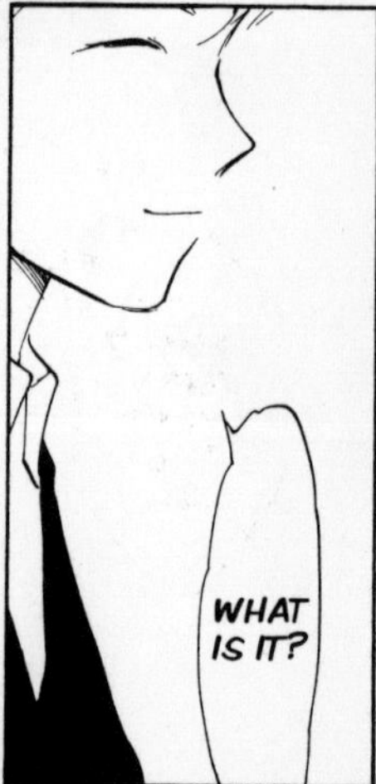
WHAT IS IT?

YOU LOOK LIKE YOU WANT TO SAY SOME-THING.

I REALIZED SOMETHING JUST NOW.
YOU KISSED ME TO TEACH ME, DIDN'T YOU?
TO TEACH ME JUST HOW...
...I FEEL ABOUT YOU.
BECAUSE I...
...WASN'T HAPPY ABOUT IT AT ALL.

THAT'S RIGHT.
I'M SORRY TO SAY...
... WHAT YOU WANTED WAS NOT A KISS FROM ME, WAS IT?
Dry lips that smelled like nothing but cigarettes.
WHY?
BUT...
BUT...
I'VE BEEN IN LOVE WITH YOU FOR SO LONG. WHY...

Why?

What hurts so much more than that is...
IKE-SHIBA-SAN.
Don't say it...
...so lightly!

I...
...MIGHT HAVE MESSED UP.
I THINK TAJIMA-KUN DESPISES ME NOW.

HUH?
RING
I...

EXCUSE ME FOR A SECOND.
RING

HISA-YOSHI-KUN?
JOLT

WHERE ARE YOU?
FIDGET FIDGET
IN FRONT OF WHAT STATION?
THAT'S FINE, BUT...
DO YOU HAVE MONEY? SPEND THE NIGHT?
FIDGET
CHARGE YOUR CELL PHONE!
EVERY-ONE'S WORRIED ABOUT YOU!
FIDGET
FIDGET
FUJIO-SAN...
WE'LL BE RUNNING THE TEST IN FIVE!
FUJIO-SAN?
OH!
YES.
FIVE MINUTES.
KLIK
IKESHIBA-SAN, WAS THAT...
YOUR AWAITED HISA-YOSHI-KUN.
He hung up though.
WHAT?
IT DOESN'T HAVE ANYTHING TO DO WITH ME.
BLUSH

DO YOU WANT TO HEAR WHAT WE TALKED ABOUT?

BLUSH

THAT'S... OKAY...

HE WAS...

...OKAY, RIGHT?

YEAH.

HEY, RIMA-CHAN, WHY DON'T YOU THINK ABOUT IT?
WHO DID YOU REALLY...
...WANT TO KISS YOU?

IKESHIBA-SAN! WORK IS MY TOP PRIORITY! KISSING?
HMM...
I DON'T WANT ANYONE TO KISS ME!
UH-HUH.
...
DID...
...TAJIMA-KUN SAY ANYTHING ABOUT ME?
NO.
SORRY TO SAY HE DIDN'T.
IS THAT SO?

FUJIO-SAN!
BUZZ
BUZZ
WE'RE READY!
FYOOO
BUZZ
OH. IKE-SHIBA-SAN!
BUZZ
HEY THERE.
BUZZ
WELL? ISN'T RIMA GREAT TODAY?
SHE IS GREAT.
SHE'S STRANGELY SEDUCTIVE.
SO YOU CAME.
UH-HUH.

I messed up.

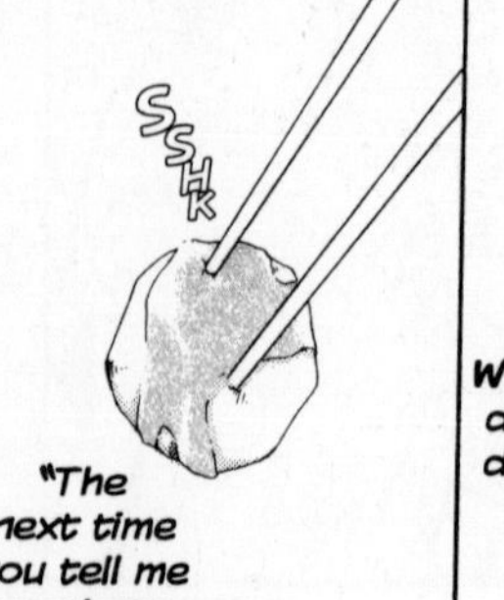
SSHK
"The next time you tell me you hate me I'll take it seriously."

What do I do?

"I hate you!"

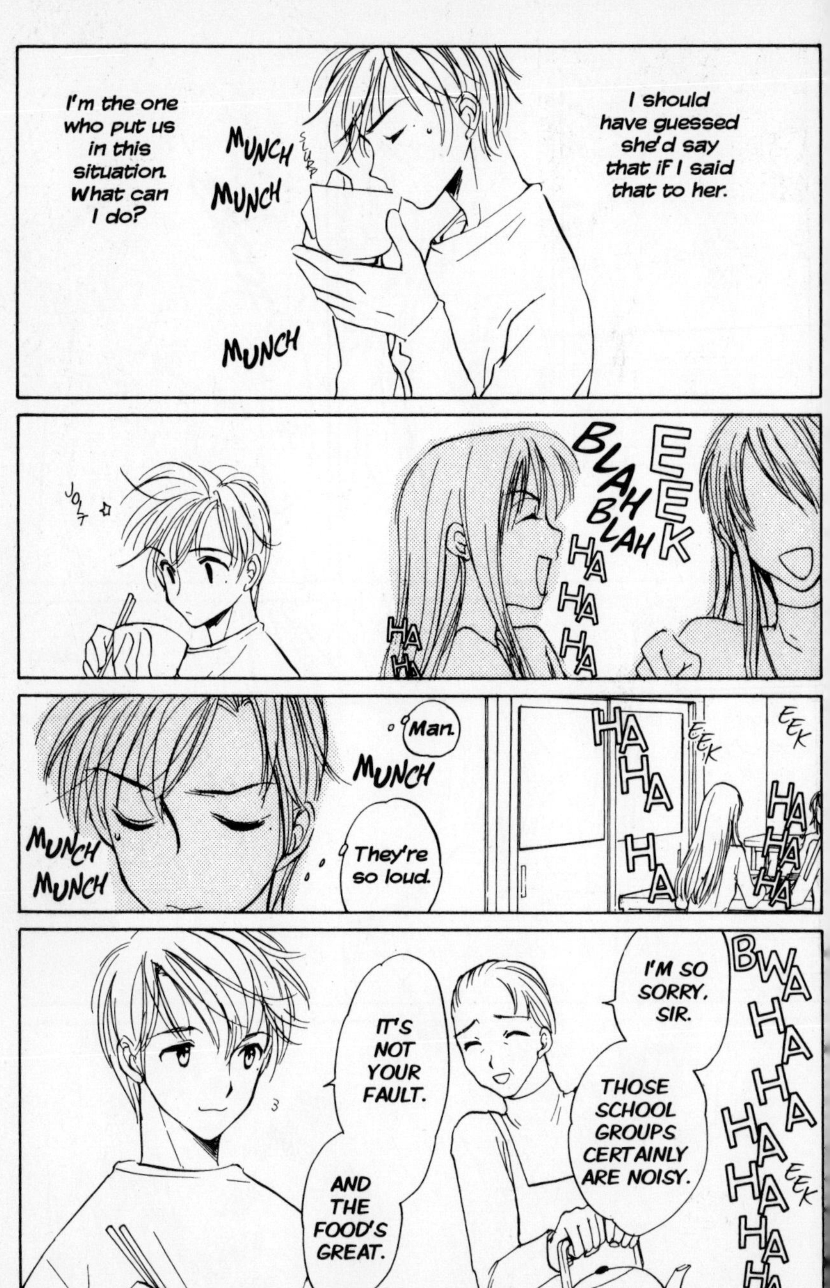
I should have guessed she'd say that if I said that to her.
I'm the one who put us in this situation. What can I do?
MUNCH
SLURP
MUNCH
MUNCH
JOLT
BLAH BLAH
EEEK
HA HA HA
HA HA
HA HA HA
EEK
EEK
HA HA HA
HA HA HA
Man.
MUNCH
They're so loud.
MUNCH MUNCH
BWA HA HA HA HA HA HA
EEK
I'M SO SORRY, SIR.
THOSE SCHOOL GROUPS CERTAINLY ARE NOISY.
IT'S NOT YOUR FAULT.
AND THE FOOD'S GREAT.

MUNCH
UM...
ARE YOU HERE ALONE?
YEP.
Do I look like I'm with someone?
WHY DON'T YOU ...
... HANG WITH US?
SORRY.
I'M OKAY FOR TODAY.
HA
HA
EEK
EEK
He totally blew us off!
EEK
HA
HA
HA
HA
Is this interest-ing for them?
What's so funny?

UM... AFTER DINNER...
...WE'RE DOING...
...FIRE-WORKS IN THE GARDEN.
COME IF YOU WANT!
THANKS.
BUT I PROBABLY WON'T.
SMILE
EEEEEK
EEEEK
It's no good!
HA HA HA
He totally blew us off!
Are they happy about it?
FOOSH

No good. If I'm the one to break, we'll be stuck in an unending cycle.

Either way it's never gonna happen.

The one in love has the weaker position.

WHY?

WHY AM I THE ONLY ONE...

...IN LOVE HERE?

Rima doesn't ...

...care
For me
at all.

FZZT
FZZ
HEY, DON'T POINT IT AT ME!
EEEK
IT'S SO SMOKY!
THIS IS THE LAST OF THE SPARKLERS, OKAY?
HEY, THAT GUY FROM EARLIER WAS PRETTY CUTE, WASN'T HE?
I FEEL LIKE I'VE SEEN HIM SOME-WHERE.
WHAT? LIKE YOU'VE MET HIM BEFORE?
NO, THAT'S NOT IT.

IZUMI INN
FZZZT
WANNA GO BACK AND WATCH DIRTY MOVIES?
THEY DIDN'T HAVE ANY!
EEK
THEY DID! ON PAY-PER-VIEW!
NO WAY!
EWW!
EEK
EEK

NOK
CAN'T SLEEP ?
KLIK

WHAT IS IT? IF YOU'RE WORRIED ABOUT SOMETHING, TALK TO YOUR MOTHER ABOUT IT.
I'M NOT.
I'M TIRED— LET ME SLEEP.
HMPH
DON'T UNDER-ESTIMATE ME.
BOY TROUBLE IS MY SPECIALTY.
JOLT
BOY TROUBLE?
HEE HEE
THAT'S RIGHT.
I'M NOT JUST SOME SLUT, YOU KNOW?
UNLIKE YOU, I'VE GOT A WEALTH OF EXPERIENCE.
FLIP

DAZE
WELL...
WHY CAN'T YOU STOP THINKING ABOUT SOME-THING YOU SAID TO SOME GUY WHEN YOU...
WELL THEN...
...HATE HIM?
HUH?
THEN YOU PROBABLY DON'T HATE HIM.
Y-
YEAH, I GUESS I DON'T HATE HIM.
FIDGET
BUT THAT DOESN'T MEAN I LIKE HIM.
FIDGET
DID YOU SAY SOME-THING TO KUMI-CHAN?
NO!
FWOOOP
I'M NOT TALKING ABOUT ME! I'M TALKING ABOUT A FRIEND! A FRIEND!
...

YOU'RE SUCH A LIAR.
YOU DON'T HAVE ANY FRIENDS TO TALK ABOUT STUFF LIKE THAT WITH.
!!
SHOCK
...
YOU'RE SO MEAN.
...
That's right, I...
I don't have any friends.

YOU WOULDN'T SPEND THAT MUCH TIME THINKING ABOUT SOMEONE YOU HATED.
THAT'S HOW WOMEN ARE.
WE'RE HEART-LESS.
I...
I'M NOT LIKE THAT.
WHAT'RE YOU TALKING ABOUT?
I WOULDN'T CALL YOU A WOMAN, RIMA!
HEH
OU'RE UST A ID! A HILD!

HA HA HA
STOP ACTING LIKE YOU'RE GROWN-UP.
GRR
MOM!
SO BASICALLY YOU'RE JEALOUS OF MY YOUTH!
WHAT WAS THAT?!
WHAT ABOUT YOU?
YOU OLD HAG!
OLD HAG!
QUIET, YOU!
Hate.. love..
It's not about that.
It's just that I can't stand thinking he despises me.

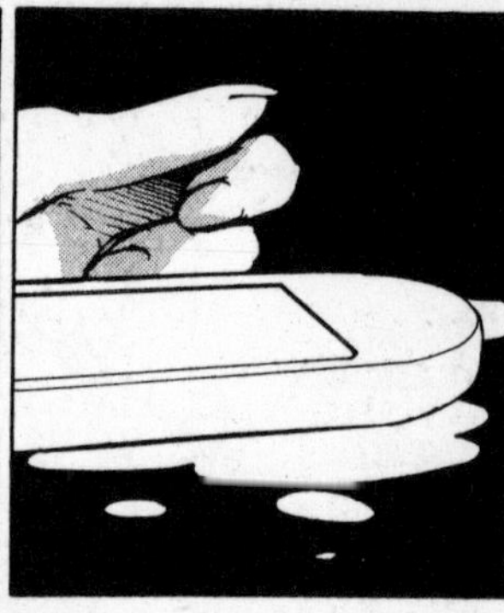

OH, HOW ARE YOU?
SORRY ABOUT THE OTHER DAY! I WENT TOO FAR!
HUH? YOU DON'T REMEMBER? NEVER MIND THEN!

No.

That would never happen.

RING
RING
RING
BEEP
HELLO?
TAJIMA-KUN? IT'S ME, FUJIO.

It'd be more like...
BEEP
HELLO?
BA
BUMP
TAJIMA-KUN? IT'S ME, FUJIO.

SULK
WHAT DO YOU WANT?
More likely...
...he'd just hang up on me or something.
YIKES
That could definitely happen!
This is the last time.
That's possible.
That's a definite possibility!
Ooh...
Oh.
I get it. That...

...was
my...
...last
chance.

"I
hate
you."

That
was my
decision.

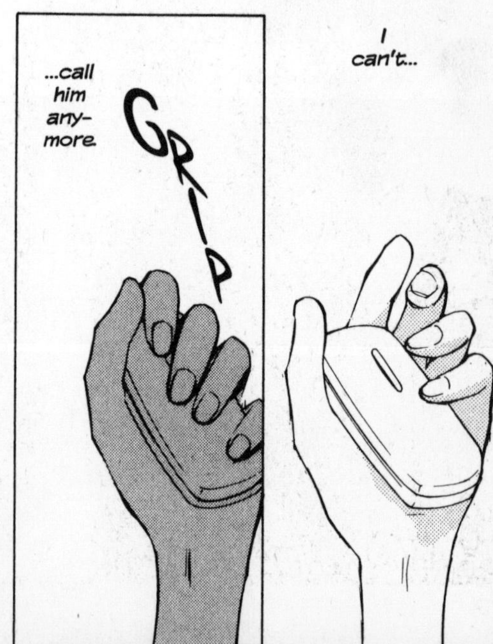
I
can't...
...call
him
any-
more.
GRIP

SPARK
KOFF
!
What is it?
?
MY THROAT HURTS.
KOFF
KOFF
SPARK
Sirens ?
WOOOOSH

WOOOSH

What is that?!
It can't be!
A Fire?
No way.
It's so hot!
What am I supposed to do in this situation?
Water?
From where?
Will I die?
I'll be okay.
If I breathe in too much smoke, I'm a goner.
I wouldn't die, right?
The fire's spread-ing...
What hap-pened...
...to every-one else?
Are they sparks?
Will I die?
Air?

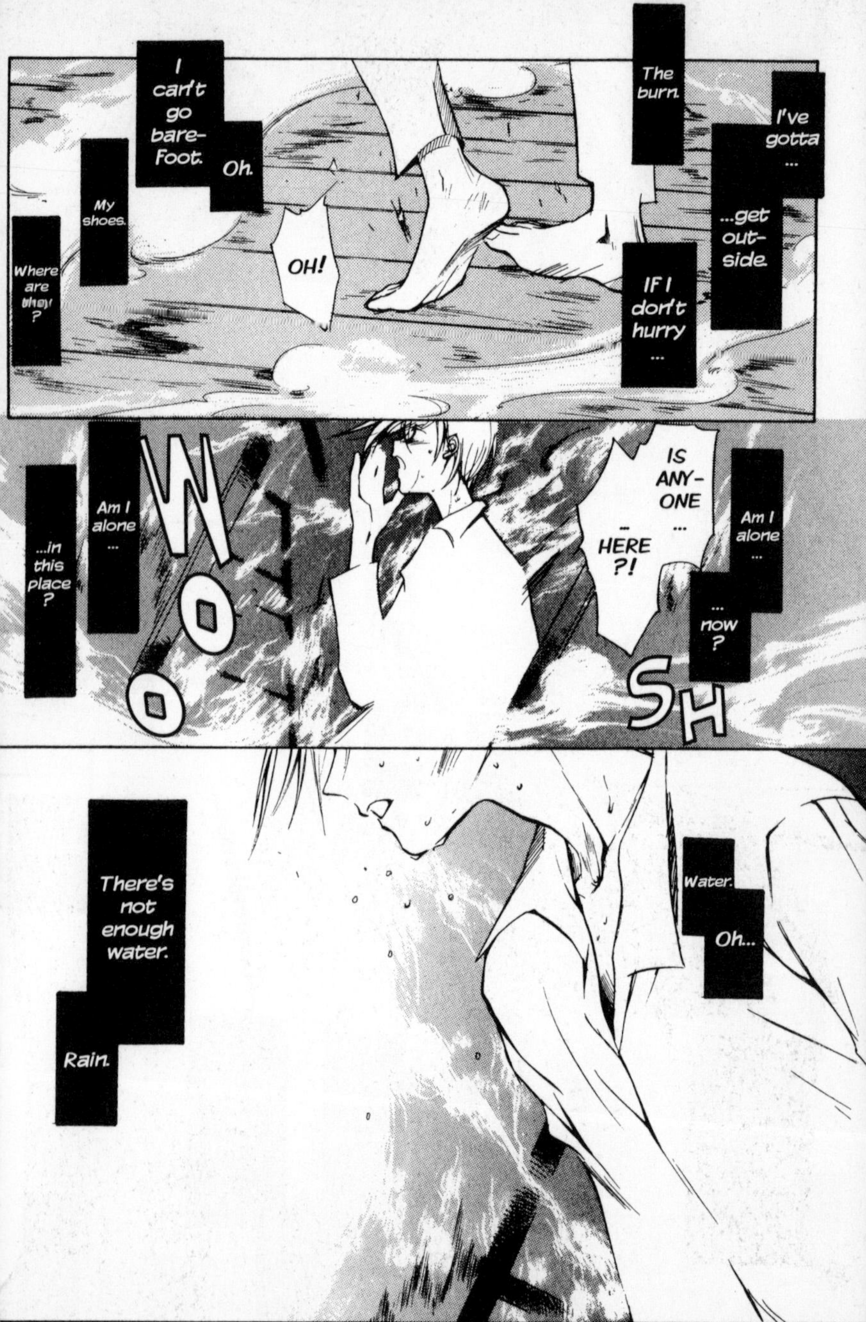
The burn.
I've gotta...
...get outside.
If I don't hurry...
OH!
Oh.
I can't go barefoot.
My shoes.
Where are they?
Am I alone...
...now?
IS ANYONE... ...HERE?!
SH
WOOO
Am I alone...
...in this place?
Water.
Oh...
There's not enough water.
Rain.

I wish it would rain.
Will I die?
From something like this?
But ...
I won't die, right?
The house isn't that big.
There's no way I can't get out.

I won't die, right?
WOO
SH
WOO
CLANG

CLANG

CLANG

WHAT DO I DO?

WHAT DO I...

PLIP

PLIP

PLIP

Even I get it.

SHOO

I would never cry over someone I hated!

He must have brainwashed me. That's it!

He was just so persistent about saying it.

"Hey, Fujio-san!"

"Yeah?"

"So have you fallen a little in love with me yet?"

"I- I'm not going to!"

"Don't answer so quickly."

What're you talking about?

What should I do?
What can I do?

"You actually like me a little, right?"
"Tajima-kun, don't you have anything else to do or think about?"
"Nope!"

I love him.
I love him so much I could die.
I can't say that. I could never say that.
I could never say that now, after everything...

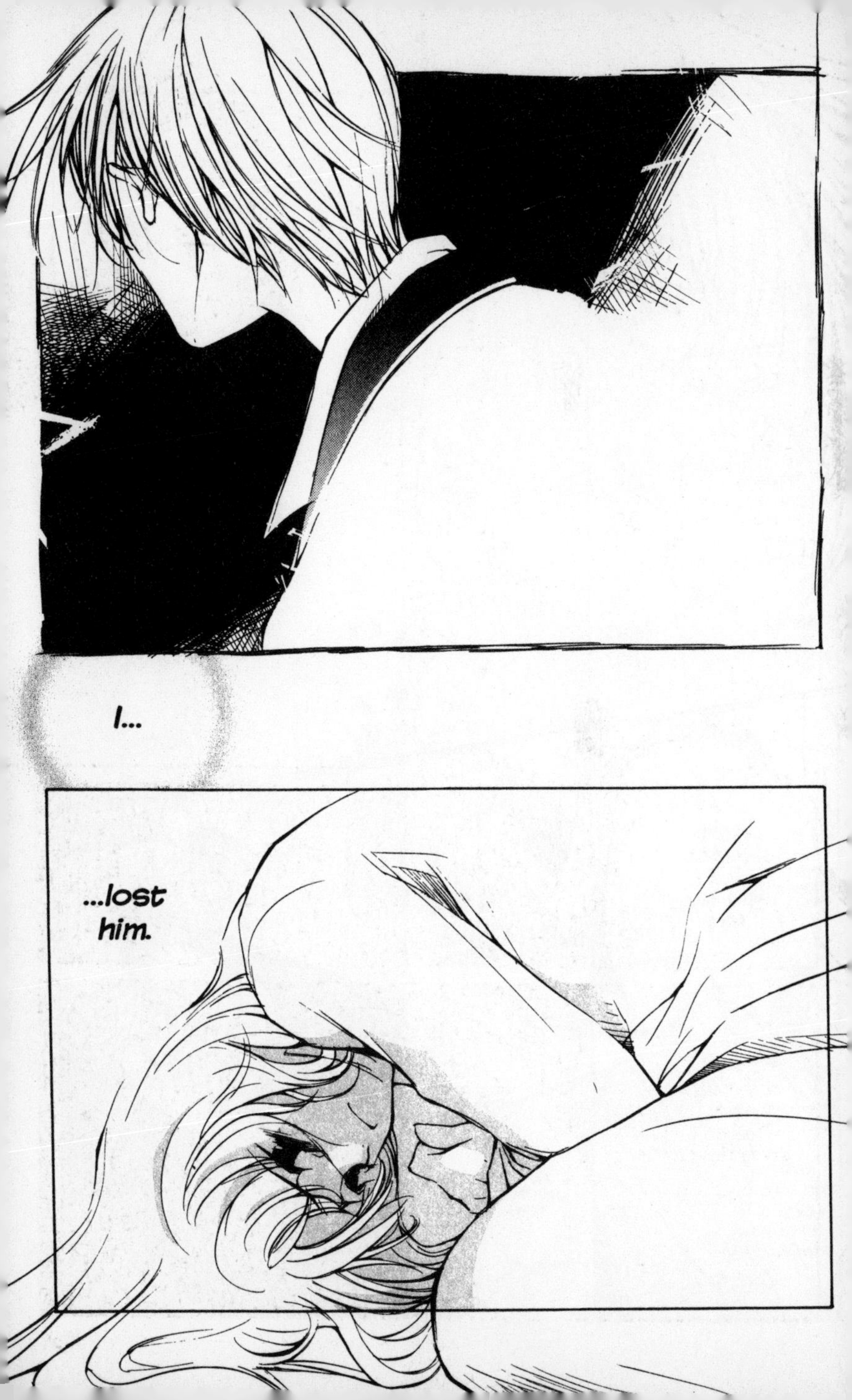

I...

...lost him.

CHECK-IN
OH MY GOSH ... IT WAS SO SCARY!
AND I'M ALL BURNED!
BUZZ BUZZ
THEY WON'T LET ME GO HOME YET.
THE CAUSE OF THE FIRE WAS...
...THE FIRE-WORKS?
AGAIN?
I THINK IT'LL BE ON THE NEWS!
YEAH.
I'M AT THE HOSPITAL NOW...
BUZZ BUZZ
AND THE FIRE ENGINES WERE KINDA...

BUZZ
DON'T CRY. YOU'RE OKAY.
BUZZ
EVEN THOUGH THE FIRE SPREAD SO QUICKLY.
IT DID.
BU
BUZZ
IT'S LUCKY NO ONE DIED!
I THOUGHT IT WAS THE END!
YOU'RE LUCKY. NONE OF YOUR BURNS ARE BAD ENOUGH TO SCAR.
BUZZ
THANK YOU.
HAVE YOU CONTACTED YOUR PARENTS?
OH...

RUB

IT DOESN'T MATTER.

BLUSH

KOFF

MY THROAT HURTS.

YOU DID INHALE SOME SMOKE.

WHY DON'T YOU LIE DOWN?

MY EYES HURT.

THEY STING.

RUB

Don't rub them!

Dawn is coming.
I didn't sleep at all tonight.
I spent the night alone waiting for morning, and now it's over.

KYOOOO

GRIP

I should go home even if things don't work out.

If they don't work out, then I can die. But I can't die until I've made sure of that.

THANK YOU FOR TAKING CARE OF ME.
THUNK
ARE YOU ALL RIGHT?
BE CARE-FUL!
SQUEAK
THANK YOU.
It's all useless.
It's useless to try to grin and bear it.
I can hold it in until it makes my stomach hurt, but it's still useless.

It's useless to try and stop myself from loving her.
I can't do it.

It'd be so much easier if I could just hate her because she hates me.
But I can't stop it even if she doesn't like me.

If I go back. I'll probably just be pathetic. It'll be really lame.

Wanting to be near her even though she acts irritated by me is just pitiful.

"I hate you!"
There's nothing I can do about it, even if she hurts me, even if she makes me cry.

I don't know why.

Is this...

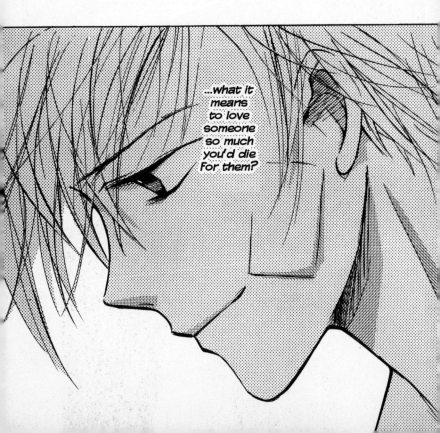

...what it means to love someone so much you'd die for them?

I wonder ...
...just how much will she take from me?
I've thrown away my pride and my vanity.
I'm totally exposed.

There's nothing inside me.
Nothing except my love for her.
Does that mean I love her enough to die for her?

I HAVEN'T SLEPT AT ALL!

TWEET

MY FACE! NOW MY FACE IS GOING TO LOOK...

MMM

I HAVE TO SLEEP, EVEN JUST FOR A LITTLE!

My-

My poor face...

I'M A PRO-FESSION-AL!

No!

I HATE YOU!

THINK REAL HARD BEFORE YOU SAY IT.

BECAUSE NEXT TIME I'LL TAKE YOU SERIOUS-LY.

No more!

Why do I keep remem-bering...
...all the things I don't want to remember!
I CAN'T SLEEP!

I DON'T REALLY HATE YOU.
Oh no.
GRIP
What am I thinking?
I LO—
N—
ZOOP
No!!
BA-BMP BA-BMP
BA-BMP
BA-BMP
There's no way I can say that now.
GULP

RING
RING
JOLT
RIIIING
BA-BMP
RIIIING
GR
AB
RING
HISAYOSHI TASHIMA
KLIK
BA-BMP
BA-BMP
HELLO
...
BA-BMP
BA-BMP
...
...
BA-BMP

BA-BMP
TH-
THIS IS TAJIMA-KUN, RIGHT?
BA-BMP
BA-BMP
WHAT?
BA-BMP

WHY... ARE YOU CALLING ME?
SAY SOME-THING.
YOU HAVE SOME-THING TO SAY, RIGHT?

I DO.
LET ME IN.

?!
I'M ...
... OUTSIDE YOUR HOUSE RIGHT NOW.
ZWIP
LET ME INSIDE.
WHAT'RE YOU TALKING ABOUT?
I DON'T BELIEVE YOU! MY MOM'S HERE!
I CAN'T LET YOU IN AT THIS TIME OF NIGHT!
I KNOW ...
... BUT ...
MITSUKO-SAN'S ASLEEP ANYWAY, RIGHT?
WELL YEAH, BUT...
...SHE MIGHT WAKE UP!
AND MORE IMPORTANT-LY, I'M IN MY PAJAMAS.

LET ME IN.
BA-BMP
BA-BMP
WHA-
WHAT DID YOU COME HERE FOR?
Y-YOU'RE NOT GOING TO DO ANYTHING WEIRD, RIGHT?
SCRATCH
I AM.

HEY ...
ARE YOU STUPID ?
I'M NOT GOING TO LET YOU IN NOW.
BLUSH
LET ME IN.
HOW COULD I LET SOMEONE WHO SAID SOMETHING LIKE THAT INSIDE?
THINK ABOUT IT, YOU IDIOT!
IDIOT.
It's not Fair.
This isn't Fair at all!

SCREECH
WHY ...
...
...ARE YOU OPENING IT?
YOU SHOULDN'T OPEN THE DOOR!
SWIP
!!!!
YOU'RE TOO SLOW.
GRAB

I CAME TO KISS YOU.
AND I'M GOING TO IF YOU LET ME INSIDE.
BLUSH
Whaaa ?!
WHA ...
ARE YOU GOING TO LET ME IN OR NOT?
WHICH IS IT?
BA-BMP
BA-BMP
WHICH IS IT?
BA-BMP

FSSH
SCREE
K'-
KEEP IT DOWN.
MY MOM REALLY WILL WAKE UP.
KLIK
KLIK

You're so mean, Tajima-kun!
Why are you putting me in such an embar-rassing situation?
JOLT
RIMA.
SHH.
TA-JIMA-KUN ...
UH ...
UM ...

What should I do?!
After everything that's happened... I can't tell him I love him now! I can't say it now!
I don't believe it. When did I fall for him?

I don't know. I can't remember. I don't believe this.

When did I fall for him?

What should I say?

You opened the door.

Oh, what do I do? Why'd I do that?
BA-BMp
BA-BMp
BA-BMp
BA-BMp
Let me inside.
But if you do...
BA-BMp
He's definitely going to kiss me.
That's what's happening.

You opened the door. That's what this means, right?
BA-BMP BA-BMP
BA-BMP BA-BMP
TA-
BA-BMP BA-BMP
JOLT
BA-BMP
YOU WANT TO HEAR IT AGAIN?
OKAY.
I'LL SAY IT AS MANY TIMES AS YOU WANT.

I LOVE YOU, RIMA.
YOU DON'T ...
...HAVE TO SAY ANYTHING.
JOLT

NO ...
TA-
GASP
GASP
TA-
TA-JIMA-KUN!
SHH.
YOU'LL WAKE UP MITSUKO-SAN.
After that...

BA-BMP
HEY.
BA-BMP
DON'T ... ... CLOSE YOUR EYES.
NO.
BA-BMP
BA-BMP
BA-BMP
HEY ...
NO ...
BA-BMP
DON'T ...
- ORDER ME AROUND.

I'M NOT.
I'M BEGGING YOU.

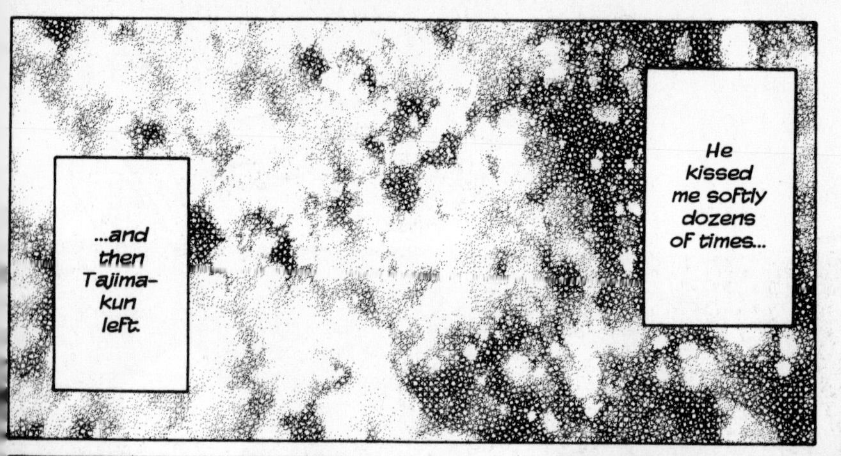

He kissed me softly dozens of times...
...and then Tajima-kun left.

It was different than kissing Ikeshiba-san.

Total-ly differ-ent.

It was only our lips touch-ing, but...

I feel so hot.

PHEW...

I MIGHT BE RUNNING A FEVER.

MORN-ING!
GOOD MORN-ING!
LISTEN TO THIS, RIMA-CHAN!
IT'S SO AMAZING ABOUT TAJIMA-KUN! HE WAS IN A FIRE ...
HUH?
IT WAS A REAL CLOSE CALL!
WHAT A SHOCK-ER!
YOU'RE OVER-REACT-ING.
YOU DON'T KNOW THAT!

GRAB
WHY ...
...DIDN'T YOU SAY SOMETHING ABOUT IT?!
UP
WHAT'S THIS INJURY?
OW!
RI—
FUJIO-SAN!
YOU SHOULD TELL PEOPLE SOMETHING THAT IMPORTANT IMMEDIATELY!
I CAN'T BELIEVE IT!

DO YOU ... HAVE ANY ...
...OTHER INJURIES?
BOP
OOF!
OUCH.
WHERE?
YEAH.
A FEW.
BOP
BOP
?
...
RIMA-CHAN?

GRRRRRR...
I—
I CAN'T BELIEVE YOU!
IDIOT!

What the–?
URGH
YOU'RE HURT...

I'M GOING TO...
SH
FWOOOO
...THE BATH-ROOM!
...
Why are you yelling?

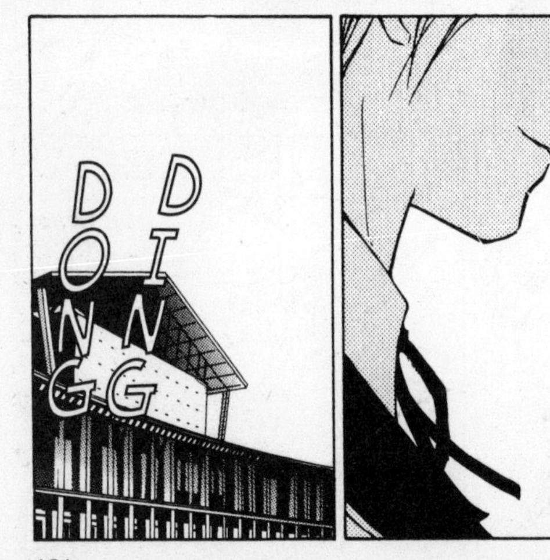
DING
DONG

FUJIO-SAN...
DON'T YOU MEAN "RIMA"?
I KNOW...
...YOU CALL ME BY MY FIRST NAME INSIDE YOUR HEAD.
...
SHOCK
WHAT ARE YOU PLANNING TO DO?
WHAT'S YOUR NEXT MOVE?
NEXT?

NOW THAT YOU'VE KISSED ME, WHAT COMES NEXT?
TAJIMA-KUN, YOU DON'T UNDER-STAND WHAT YOU DID.
As if Tajima-kun would understand.
As if he'd understand how I feel.
My lips are the door that leads to every-thing else.

Tajima-kun opened that door.

I DO UNDERSTAND!

THUNK
I'LL GIVE YOU ALL OF ME.
YOU MEAN YOU'LL BE MINE?
THUNK
I MEAN I'LL BE YOURS. RIMA.
My fingers tingled at those words.

Does your First love turn you stupid?
HAS FUJIO-SAN COME IN?
SORRY, NOT YET.
SWOOP
SWOOP
SHE'LL BE HERE SOON.
WHAT?
WILL THIS BE ALL RIGHT?
I-
RUSH
I'M SORRY!
I'M SO SORRY.
YEEK
SHEESH!
YOU'RE LATE, RIMA-CHAN!

We didn't do anything.

We were just together.

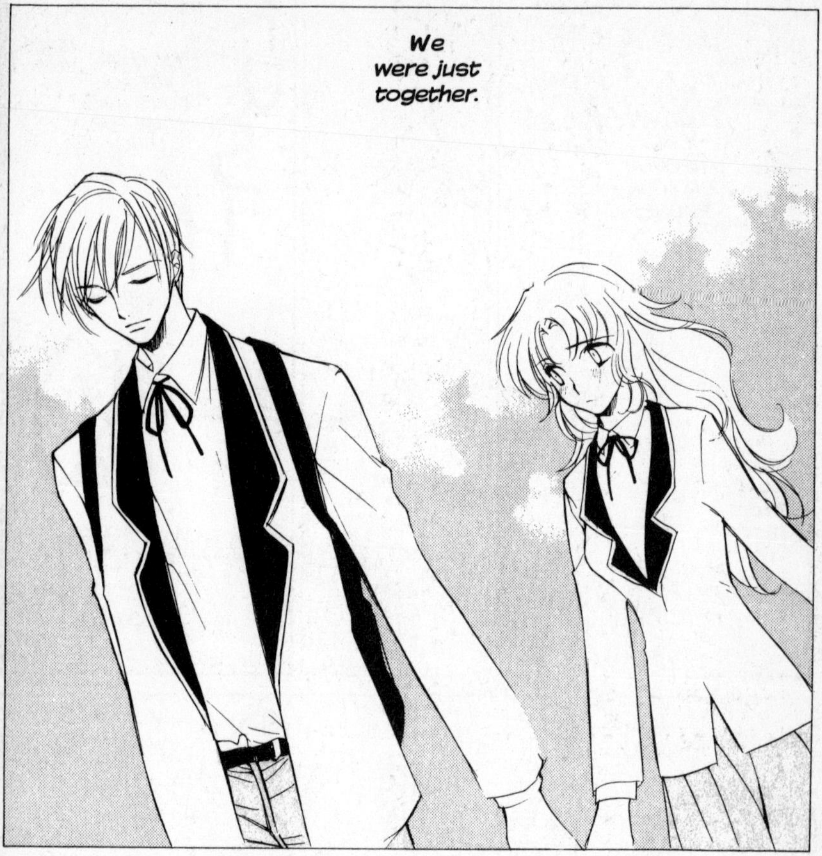

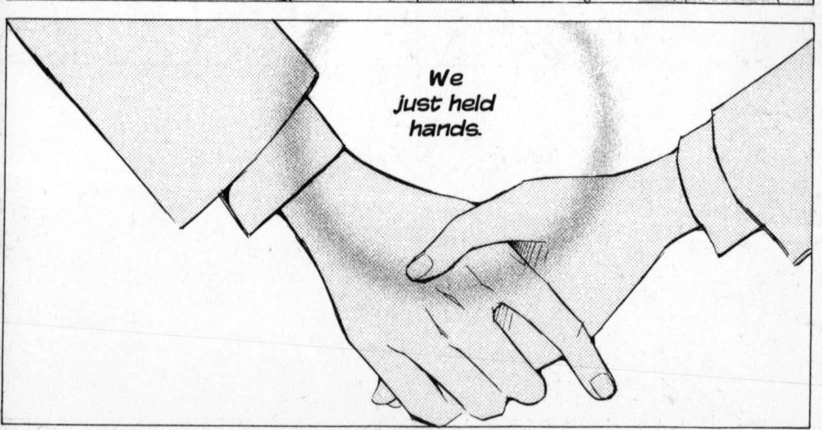
We just held hands.

All right then, next question! Rima-chan, when was your first love?
Oh, when I was in preschool.
In preschool? That's so typical.
Yep. And then I went to elementary school...
Oh.
I had a real crush in third grade and... sixth grade.
So how about now?
Now my boyfriend is my job.
Spoken like a Goody Two-shoes!
HA HA HA
That was all wrong.
Everything I thought was love until now...
I was wrong about all of it.

YOU KNOW, THIS IS MY FIRST LOVE.

YOU'RE MY FIRST LOVE, RIMA.

WHAT ABOUT YOU?
ME...
ME TOO.

REALLY?
THAT'S AMAZ-ING.
THEY ALWAYS SAY YOUR FIRST LOVE NEVER FADES.
RIGHT?

BUT I WAS REALLY YOUR FIRST LOVE?
MM...
It's true. This is a first for me.

I Feel like I'm melting.

DID SOMETHING HAPPEN?
It's not anything about my first love...
Actually...
N—
NO—
Really...
BLUSH
NOTHING HAPPENED.
I'm just turning into an idiot!!

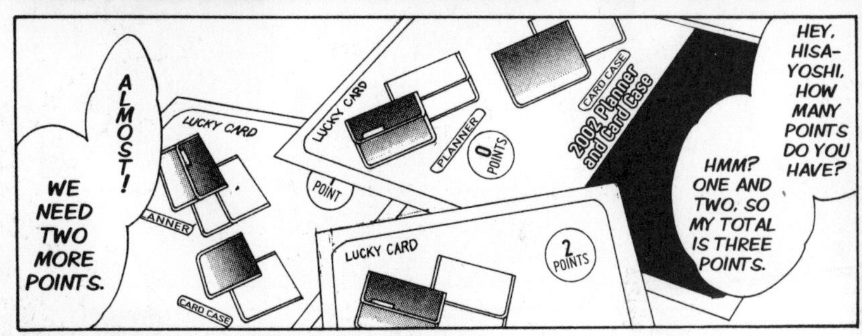

HEY, HISA-YOSHI, HOW MANY POINTS DO YOU HAVE?
HMM? ONE AND TWO, SO MY TOTAL IS THREE POINTS.
2002 Planner and Card Case
CARD CASE
PLANNER
LUCKY CARD
0 POINTS
1 POINT
2 POINTS
ALMOST!
WE NEED TWO MORE POINTS.

MR. DONUTS POINT CARDS ARE SO ADDICTIVE.

THEY ARE!

IT'S SO CUTE!

I WANT IT!

DARN IT, ONLY TWO POINTS!

I'M...

...SCARED.

OF WHAT?

\Huh?/

MY-SELF.

WHEN IT COMES TO RIMA, I ACT LIKE A STALKER.
I DO THINGS THAT SHE SHOULD HATE ME FOR.

HUH?

IT'S KIND OF LATE FOR THAT!
HISAYOSHI, YOU'VE BEEN ACTING LIKE A STALKER FROM THE VERY BEGIN-NING!
THAT'S ...
...REALLY BAD!

YOU'RE NOT GOING TO LIKE ANY-THING SOMEONE DOES IF YOU HATE THEM.
But you like whatever someone you love does. That's how it is.
OOH, JUST TWO MORE POINTS...
STARTS DEC. 5

But you like whatever...
SHINGO...
...someone you love does.
YOU'RE AMAZING.
DID YOU JUST REALIZE THAT NOW?
PEACE
CLAP
CLAP
HOW ABOUT I EAT THREE MORE DOUGHNUTS?
WE MIGHT GET THOSE TWO POINTS.
SERIOUSLY?
I'VE REACHED MY LIMIT.
I'M COUNTING ON YOU!
But...
...Shingo is...

..just a kid.
I get greedier and greedier.
I an't do nything bout it.
At First it was enough to just see her.
It was enough just to hear her voice.
Then our eyes met, and she remembered my name...
...and I wanted her to call me by it.
I want to talk to her more.
I want to be with her more.

I want to touch her more.

HISA-YOSHI?

YEAH.

JOLT

WHAT'RE YOU SPACING OUT FOR?

YOUR DOUGH-NUTS!

Eat them.

I bought them, so you have to eat them.

OH.

YEAH, OKAY.

Wait a second. More? I can't do more than that...

WHA?

?

I DUNNO.

IT'S JUST A FEELING.

I'M NOT LIKE THAT.

BUT YOU KNOW.

I THINK...

THUNK

ODDLY ENOUGH...

...RIMA MIGHT HAVE LIKED YOU FOR A WHILE.

JOLT

WITH ME, IT'S MORE LIKE WE STARTED OUT AS FRIENDS AND BEFORE WE REALIZED IT...
RING RING RING
OH...
...MY PHONE.
That sounds ...
...too good to be true.
MANA? IT'S ME.
TONIGHT? I'M THERE!
YEAH.
MAKE ODEN FOR DINNER, OKAY?
I'D LOVE ODEN. ♥
Shingo makes me jealous.
We're a little awkward.

AND THAT'S IT.
THIS WILL BE OUR SCHEDULE UP UNTIL THE RELEASE DATE.
BUZZ
DOES ANYONE HAVE ANY QUES-TIONS?
THUNK
RM
ALL RIGHT.
THEN WE'RE DONE.
I'M GOING TO ORDER CATER-ING.
PASS THE MENU AROUND.
Good work!
OH, I'M...
...GOING HO—
SWIP
RIMA-CHAN.
THE PRESI-DENT...
HUH?
JOLT
...SAYS TO EAT WITH HER ONCE IN A WHILE.
PRESIDENT

THESE BOXED LUNCHES ARE SO GOOD.

I REALLY LIKE THEM.

HOW ABOUT YOU, RIMA-CHAN?

YES!

I LIKE THEM TOO.

Aww...

I do, but... I wanted to go home early today.

I want to go home and eat with Tajima—

CHOMP

YOU'VE BEEN LOOKING SO CUTE LATELY.

DID ANYTHING HAPPEN?

BA-BMP
BA-BMP
YOU THINK SO? I'M SO HAPPY!
I'M ON THIS HARD-CORE DIET.
BA-BMP
I GUESS IT'S WORKING.
BA-BMP
BA-BMP

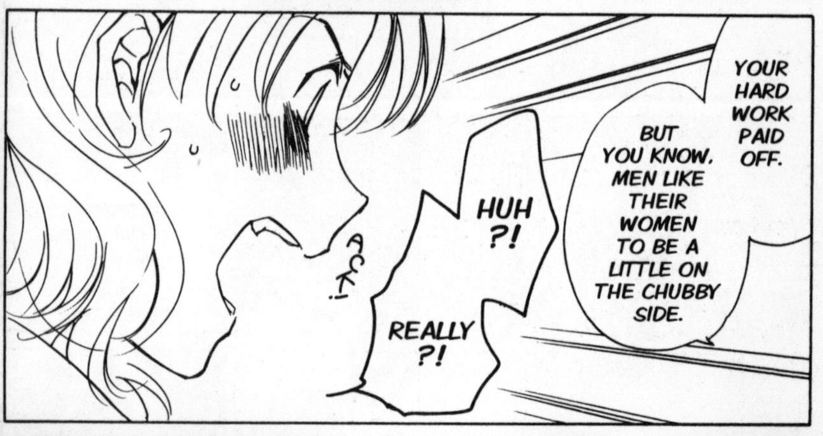

MUNCH
MUNCH
MUNCH
... ...
...

UM ... SO ...
I GUESS GUYS LIKE...
MUNCH
...PERKY BREASTS AND STUFF?
MUNCH
OF COURSE.

SO THERE IS A GUY.
NO!
HAVING PERKY BREASTS IS ALSO PART OF MY JOB!
IS IT?

I SEE.
THAT'S TRUE.
A NORMAL 17-YEAR-OLD GIRL...
...WOULD NEVER HAVE TO CHOOSE BETWEEN...
...LOVE AND WORK, RIGHT?
SMILE
WHICH WOULD YOU CHOOSE, RIMA-CHAN?
...
BOTH.
I MEAN, WHEN I CAN'T DECIDE WHICH CAKE TO GET, I EAT BOTH.
HMM...

I'M GLAD YOU GAVE SUCH A NON-COMMITAL ANSWER.
IT WOULDN'T BE VERY CUTE OF YOU TO SAY WORK.

AND I'D BE DISAPPOINTED IF YOU SAID LOVE.
...

WANT ME TO GIVE YOU A TIP? IF YOU FOCUS ONLY ON WORK...
...YOU TURN OUT LIKE ME.
SIGH
AND ...

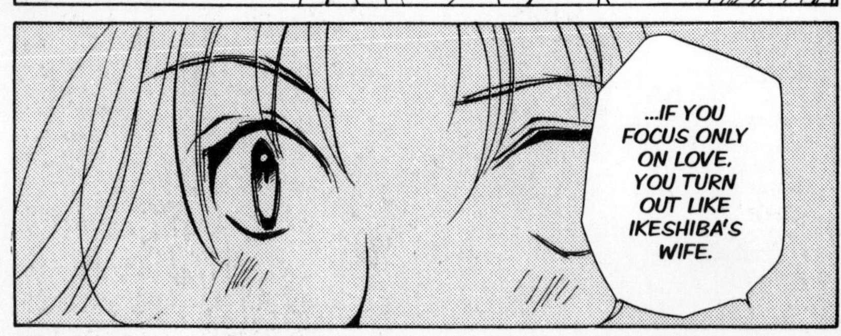
...IF YOU FOCUS ONLY ON LOVE, YOU TURN OUT LIKE IKESHIBA'S WIFE.

YOU KNOW ABOUT HER, RIGHT?
I...
I HEARD SHE'S IN THE HOSPITAL.
IT'S MORE OF A TREATMENT CENTER THAN A HOSPITAL.
SHE LOVED IKESHIBA A LITTLE TOO MUCH, AND SHE HAD A BIT OF A BREAKDOWN.
SHE WAS MARRIED WITH A CHILD, SO WHAT WAS SHE SO AFRAID OF?
THERE'S NOTHING BETWEEN IKESHIBA AND ME.
IKESHIBA-SAN'S WIFE...
...WAS SUSPICIOUS OF YOU AND IKESHIBA-SAN?
THE SIMPLE ANSWER IS YES.
AFTER ALL, OUR JOB IS WHAT IT IS. THAT WASN'T EVERYTHING, BUT YES.

DESTROYING YOURSELF WITH SUSPICIONS OVER A RELATIONSHIP THAT DOESN'T EXIST.
DE-STROYING YOURSELF BECAUSE YOU LOVE SOMEONE TOO MUCH.
LOVE IS ALSO A FIGHT AGAINST YOUR-SELF.

Self...
...de-struction.

A fight against yourself?

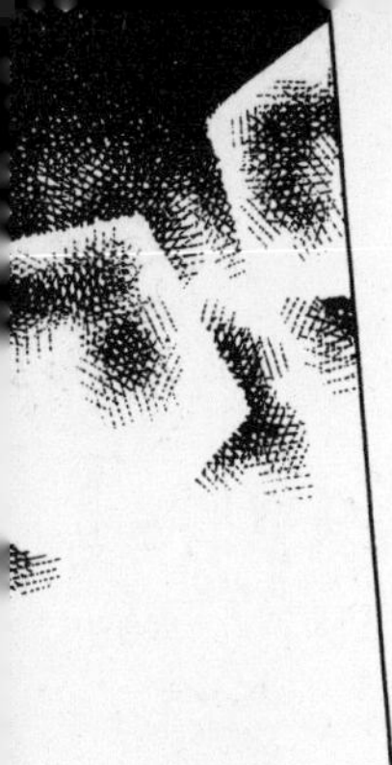

It's strange.

When I think about him...

...it makes my chest hurt.

It hurts so much...

...just thinking of him...

...that I feel like I'm going to die.

WELL... JUST PRACTICE MODERATION.

FOR NOW, I JUST WANT TO MAKE THAT CLEAR.

PRESIDENT!

YES?

WAS THERE REALLY NOTHING BETWEEN YOU AND IKESHIBA-SAN?

NOTHING.

IF THERE WAS, WE'D NEVER BE ABLE TO WORK TOGETHER ALL THIS TIME.

GLANCE

I KISSED HIM.

WHAT?

I KISSED IKESHIBA-SAN.
BUT THE ONLY THING THAT HAPPENED WAS THAT I KNEW I DIDN'T LOVE HIM.
I'M NOT ... ... GOING TO...
...DE-STROY MYSELF.
IF I FALL FOR HIM SO HARD THAT IT BREAKS ME DOWN...
SHF
I'LL...
...LAY IT ALL ON TAJIMA-KUN.
BEEEP

BECAUSE THAT'S WHAT HE'S ALWAYS DONE TO ME.
THROB THROB
...
SLUMP
SO IT IS HISA-YOSHI TAJIMA THEN.
YES! IT'S TAJIMA-KUN!
RING
HEY, HISA-YOSHI!
WHO IS IT?
IT'S RIMA!

TA-JIMA-KUN? IT'S RIMA. COME MEET ME AT THE OFFICE RIGHT AWAY.
THE PRESI-DENT IS MAD AT ME.

SHE WANTS US TO BREAK UP.

WHA?!

YEAH, THAT'S RIGHT.

WHAT SHOULD WE DO? SHOULD WE BREAK UP?

I didn't go that far...

That has a nice ring to it.

The only way we can break up...
...is if we're in a relationship!
THROB
WAIT UP, I'LL BE RIGHT THERE.
I WON'T BREAK UP NO MATTER WHAT.
IF WE DO BREAK UP...
I WANT YOU TO DUMP ME WHEN YOU START TO HATE ME.

IT'S KIND OF A SIMPLE THING, BUT...
AHEM
YOU SEEMED LIKE A PRINCE TO ME.
I called him...
...to say, "Come right away."
I'm so happy.

To say, "Protect me."
I never thought...
...I'd do something so embar-rassing.
FUJIO-SAN AND I...
... ARE DAT-ING.
WHAT WAS THAT?
IS THAT TRUE?
GRIP
ARE YOU SERIOUS?
I'M SERIOUS!

BLUSH
IF...
... I'VE ...
...BECOME A PRINCE...
...IT'S ALL BECAUSE OF YOU, RIMA.
BECAUSE YOU'RE A PRINCESS.

You make me a princess...

...and come to my rescue wherever I am?

It's so strange to think someone like that exists.

To think that there's someone who fills my heart this way.

OOH ...
MY HEAD HURTS.
WHAT IS GOING ON, IKESHIBA-KUN? WHAT ARE WE GOING TO DO ABOUT THIS?
I KNOW, RIGHT?
THUNK
DON'T GIVE ME THAT!
THIS IS A SCANDAL!
FUJIO WAS SAYING SOMETHING ABOUT YOU KISSING HER.
GLARE
WHAT DID SHE MEAN BY THAT?
WHAT EXACTLY COULD SHE MEAN? I DON'T KNOW.
THAT'S THE KIND OF ATTITUDE THAT GAVE YOUR WIFE HER NERVOUS CONDITION!
ACK.
TURN THE KNIFE AND TWIST IT.
ALTHOUGH ...
...
IT'S TRUE.
I'M A FAILURE OF A MAN, UNABLE TO EVEN PROTECT MY OWN WIFE.

THAT'S ENOUGH.
I'VE NEVER FALLEN IN LOVE AND THAT'S WHY I'VE BEEN ABLE TO BE WITH YOU...
SQUEAK
...ALL THIS TIME.
I WANT TO TELL THOSE FOOLISH, LOVESICK KIDS...
SIGH
...IT'S BETTER NEVER TO FALL IN LOVE.
...
STARE
?
I WONDER IF THIS IS...
...WHAT THEY CALL THE AFTER-GLOW.
SIGH
WE WOULDN'T GO THAT FAR.
AND THAT WORD MEANS SOMETHING A LOT MORE EMBARRAS-SING THAN YOU THINK.

KLIK
FUJIO-SAN, RIGHT? I'M FROM THE WEEKLY SCOOP...
COULD WE TALK?
!!
KLIK
IS THAT ...
... YOUR BOY-FRIEND?
WAIT A MINUTE, YOU...
DON'T!
TA-JIMA-KUN.

YOU SEEM REALLY CLOSE.
ARE YOU DATING?
What... What wa...
What am I supposed to do here?
T—
T—
TAJIMA-KUN, WAIT.
THAT'S OUR BUSINESS.
IT HAS NOTHING TO DO WITH YOU.
GRIP
GRIP
WE'VE DONE NOTHING TO BE ASHAMED OF!

WE'RE... ...SERIOUS.
WE'RE PUTTING EVERYTHING WE'VE GOT INTO THIS RELATIONSHIP.
I WON'T LET ANYONE GIVE US TROUBLE ABOUT IT.
DATING.
IS THAT TRUE, FUJIO-SAN?
YOU ADMIT IT?
...
IS THAT SO? FUJIO-SAN?
I...
I...
It's easy to tell a lie that no one will believe, but...
But...
THIS MAN...

I LOVE ...
... THIS MAN.
I don't want to cheapen it.
I LOVE HIM MORE THAN ANY-THING IN THE WORLD.
Don't ever let go of my hand.
Keep hold of each other no matter what.

I don't want to cheapen this.
WHAT?! NO WAY!
FOR REAL?
RIMA FUJIO'S GOT A BOY-FRIEND!
WOW...
OF COURSE SHE DOES.
I DON'T BELIEVE IT!
YOU SERIOUS?
WHAT A BUMMER.
HOW OLD IS FUJIO AGAIN?
HER BOY-FRIEND'S PRETTY HOT!
YOU WANT TO ASK ABOUT THAT?
I CAN'T PUT YOU DIRECTLY THROUGH TO HER.
WHAT?!
RING
RING
RIIING
AN INTERVIEW ABOUT HER ADMITTING SHE HAS A BOY-FRIEND?
NO, WE CAN'T DO THAT.
RIMA FUJIO IS MADLY IN LO
MIDNIGHT DATING?

SILENCE

SHIVER SHIVER
SHIVER

THOSE TWO ARE SO STUPID.
THEY SHOULD HAVE SAID THEY WERE JUST FRIENDS.
PSST
NEVER HAPPEN.
THEY'RE NOT THE TYPE.
THAT'S TRUE, BUT STILL ...

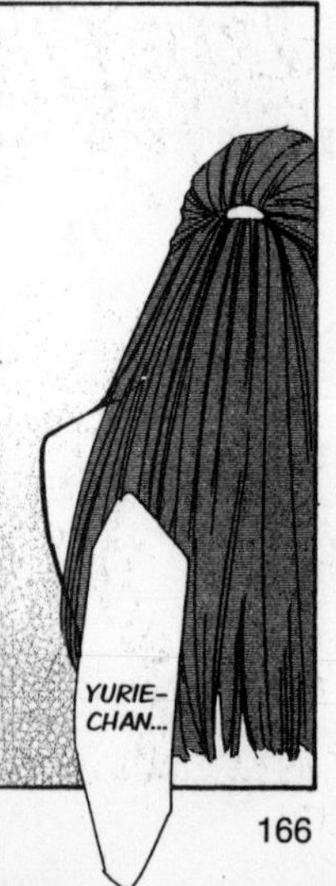
YURIE-CHAN...

WHAT DO YOU THINK SHE'LL DO ?
WELL.. BASED ON HER PERSONALITY, SHE'LL PROBABLY FIGHT WITH RIMA.
PST
YEAH.
SHE WON'T GO TO KUMI-CHAN.
PST PST

...
THUNK
JOLT

THERE'S SOMETHING I NEED TO ASK YOU!
BUT ... I DON'T HAVE THE RIGHT TO BUTT INTO YOUR BUSINESS...
SO YOU CAN TELL ME TO BUTT OUT.
RUN AWAY IF YOU WANT!
I WON'T RUN.
I'LL ANSWER ANYTHING YOU WANT.
YOU SAID...
...YOU WEREN'T IN LOVE WITH TAJIMA-KUN!
YOU SAID YOU'D NEVER FALL FOR HIM!

I DID SAY THAT.

BUT ...

I FELL FOR HIM. SORRY.

THAT'S NOT FAIR.

I'VE BEEN IN LOVE WITH HIM WAY LONGER!

AND NOW YOU ...

I'M SORRY.

BUT I...

...WON'T GIVE HIM UP TO ANYONE.

FUJIO-SAN, YOU...
...HURT TAJIMA-KUN SO BADLY!
YOU GOT IN HIS WAY. YOU TOYED WITH HIM...
YOU DON'T DESERVE HIM.
I'D BE SO MUCH BETTER FOR HIM.

We've got nothing to lose or protect.

We've got nothing except our sincerity.

Other people and adults might laugh at it...

But I'm going to use my sincerity...

NO.

I WON'T LET ANYONE ELSE HAVE TAJIMA-KUN.

HE'S MINE.

...to crush her sincerity.

You only...

...love once. Just once.

I WON'T GIVE UP A SINGLE PIECE OF HIM.

I'M NOT GIVING UP.

I'LL STEAL HIM FROM YOU ONE DAY.

Only one person, even if they never love you back...

YOU'RE AN IDIOT... ...HISA-YOSHI.
YOU THINK SO TOO?

OF COURSE.
THERE ARE SO MANY BETTER WAYS YOU COULD HAVE DONE IT.
A HA HA!
OOH...
TAJIMA-KUN'S PROFILE IS OUT TOO!
TwinKLe

I DON'T MIND. IT'S JUST, RIMA'S JOB...
YEAH, REALLY.
UH.
UMM ...
I MEAN, RIMA REALLY LOVES HER JOB...
I'M A BOTHER.
YEAH, REALLY.
SHINGO!

I FEEL SO HELPLESS.
EVEN IF I GIVE HER EVERYTHING, I'M STILL LACKING.

YOU'RE NOT LACKING.
EVEN YOU DON'T REALLY THINK THAT.

HUH?
SMILE♡
YOU THINK SO?

I'M ONLY TELLING YOU THIS, SHINGO.
PST
WHAT? WHAT?
NO FAIR!
WHAT IS IT?
IT'S GUY TALK.

WHAAT? ARE YOU SERIOUS?
IT'S COMPLETELY TRUE.
WHOA!
WOW.
WHAT?

HEH
HEH
THAT'S AMAZING!
TELL ME!
C'MON, WHAT!
SHH...

YEAH.
THERE'S A REPORTER HERE.
THEY'RE STAKING ME OUT. YOU SHOULDN'T COME OVER TODAY.
YEAH ... YEAH.
BYE THEN.
GOOD NIGHT.

OOOOH.
LOOK AT YOU BRAZENLY MAKING A ROMANTIC PHONE CALL!
JOLT
AHH!
STOP LISTENING IN!

HMM.
WHAT ARE YOU GOING TO DO WITH YOURSELF NOW?
I...
I'M NOT GOING TO DO ANY-THING.
NOTH-ING.

I LOVE SINGING.
AND I LOVE TAJIMA-KUN.
IT'S OBVIOUS. I'M GOING TO CHOOSE BOTH.
THEY WON'T LET YOU HAVE BOTH, YOU KNOW.
SOCIETY! YOUR FANS!
Hee hee hee
GRRR
I'LL CROSS THAT BRIDGE WHEN I COME TO IT!
I'M NOT GOING TO GIVE UP BEFORE ANYTHING'S HAPPENED!
THIS IS MY LIFE, SO...
...I WANT TO DO WHAT I LOVE AND BE HAPPY.
I'M GOING TO GIVE LIFE EVERYTHING I'VE GOT.
RIMA!
HUG
W- WHAT?

YOU'RE SO GOOD TO YOUR MOTHER!

AS LONG AS YOU'RE HAPPY, I'M HAPPY.

Y IN LOVE!

CLINK

SO... WHAT'S THIS?

YOU REALLY ARE... ...SOMETHING ELSE.

I'M IMPRESSED THAT YOU CAME TO APOLOGIZE, BUT...

SIGH

UM...

I DIDN'T COME HERE TO APOLOGIZE OR ANYTHING.

I CAME TO ANNOUNCE SOMETHING.

CLINK

I'M GOING TO MARRY RIMA FUJIO.

WHA-

MARRY ?!

HISA-YOSHI-SAN.

YOU BRAT...

I KNEW THAT WOULD BE YOUR REACTION!

YOU'RE 17 YEARS OLD.

WE'RE GETTING MARRIED NEXT YEAR, WHEN I TURN 18.

THIS DECISION LASTS YOUR WHOLE LIFE. DON'T MAKE IT SO LIGHTLY.

I DIDN'T MAKE IT LIGHTLY!

I'M SERIOUS.

PROBABLY AS MUCH AS YOU WERE WHEN YOU DECIDED TO GET MARRIED.

I TOLD YOU, DIDN'T I?
I CAME TO MAKE AN ANNOUNCE-MENT.
I DIDN'T COME TO GET YOUR PERMISSION.
HISA-YOSHI.
KLINK
YOU LITTLE ...
BUT...
HOW ...
HOW COULD I UNDER-STAND THAT?
BLUSH
I REALLY DO WANT YOUR BLESS-ING.
PLEASE UNDER-STAND, DAD.
I'M ONLY ...
...SAYING THIS BECAUSE I'M FOND OF YOU!

THANK YOU... SO MUCH.
MY HEAD HURTS.
WHAT WITH ALL OF THIS HAPPENING...
SIGH
IS THAT SO?
WOULD YOU LIKE SOME COFFEE?
...
HOW CAN YOU ACT SO CALM?
IT'S NOT LIKE SHE'S LOST ANY WORK.
HMM.
SHF
ON THE CONTRARY, SHE'S GETTING EVEN MORE FAN LETTERS WISHING HER LUCK.

IDOLS AREN'T DOLLS NOWADAYS ...
...
PEOPLE LOOK AT THE WAY THEY LIVE THEIR LIVES.

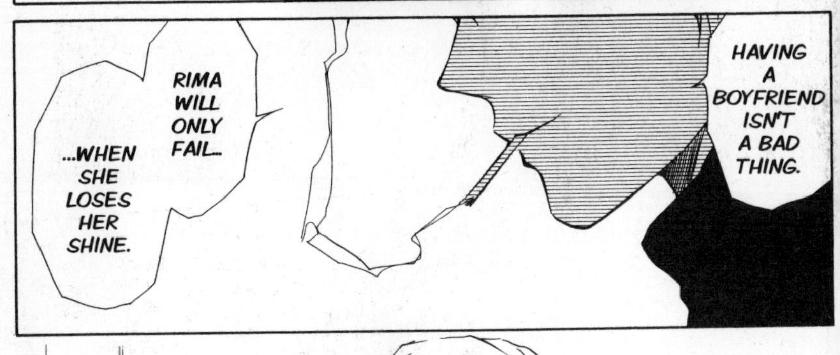

HAVING A BOYFRIEND ISN'T A BAD THING.
RIMA WILL ONLY FAIL...
...WHEN SHE LOSES HER SHINE.

YOU SAID IT'S BETTER NOT TO FALL IN LOVE BUT...

THOSE KIDS...

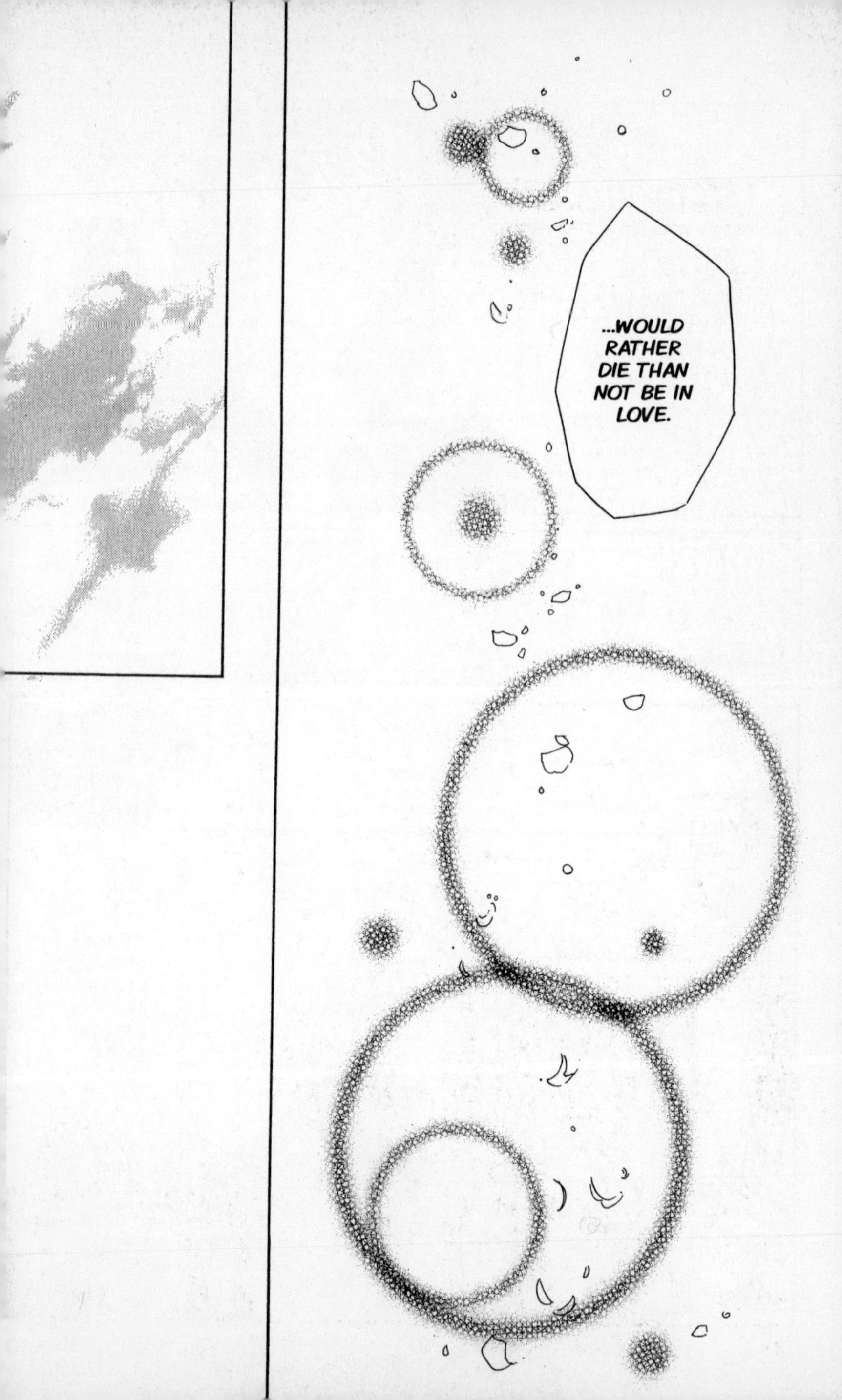
...WOULD RATHER DIE THAN NOT BE IN LOVE.

I'll love you with everything I've got.
IF people want to laugh and call it puppy love, let them laugh.

GOOD MORNING, TAJIMA-KUN!
MORNING!
TWEET
DO YOU HAVE YOUR LUNCH?
YEAH.
I DIDN'T GET TO STUDY AT ALL FOR THE TEST TODAY!
OOH, UH... WELL, WE CAN'T HELP THAT.
JUST DO YOUR BEST WHEN YOU RETAKE IT.
SIGH
WAAAAA!
I'LL TEACH YOU, SO IT'LL BE FINE.
O— OKAY.
...
TMP
TMP
TMP
PST
HEY.
HEY...
I CAN'T WAIT TO GET MARRIED.

Even my Future.

CROWN OF LOVE VOL. 4 END

AFTERWORD.

Thanks! ♥

–Yuri Kouga

April 2002

CROWN OF LOVE...
...IS DONE!
IT'S...
CLAP CLAP
CLAP CLAP
... DONE!

Oh.
My greeting is done.
What do I do?
It's not done!
You've got three pages to go!
BUZZ ZZZ

THANK YOU SO MUCH FOR STICKING WITH IT THIS WHOLE TIME! I HOPE I GET A CHANCE TO SEE YOU ALL AGAIN SOON! THANKS!

TALKING ABOUT LOVE

To tell the truth (to tell it?) I really kind of (kind of?) totally love to hear about other people's relationships.
Cuz it's cute!
So this guy came to pick me up in a convertible on Christmas Eve...
For real?!
For real! And he brought wine!
No way. It's like the '80s!
Amazing.
It was cold.
Well, that's okay.
It wasn't okay!
back
TREMBLE

Risa-chan, you draw manga, right?
How about drawing something like that?
IMPOSSIBLE.
I can't use something like that.
BLUNT
There's not much I can use in my manga. (It's never as interesting as they think it is.)
It's interesting to me because they're my friends, but if they weren't, it'd be nothing special.

If you think about it, people are total idiots when they're in love.

Including myself, of course.

Mangaka are also total idiots when they're drawing manga.
When I'm drawing, I'm totally frantic. I don't understand things like stupidity or embarrassment... (I don't notice it.)
Ooooh!
What?
Do-
Do people really say stuff like this?
Or even think it?
I don't believe it.

It's okay, Tajima-kun...
I love your embarrassing side.
...

Things that aren't anything important, or things that would freak you out if someone actually said them to you...

All of that becomes really important.

It's funny.

I wonder where the excitement comes from?
BUZZ

But I guess a life without excitement, without embarrassment, without any pain...

...would be a really boring one, so I don't mind being an idiot.

Thank-you corner for my staff.

HIROE-CHAN! TAMA-SAN!
TOBARIN! CHOFU!
OZAKI-SAN! SHIMA-CHAN!
SHIHO! HIMARI! KURI-SAN!
TENKO! SEI-CHAN!
YOSSAN!

And Kaminaga-sama, Iwahashi-sama, Sekiguchi-sama, Yamada-sama.

This manga has been assisted by at least three generations of Kouga's assistants.
Thank you so much!

Crown of Love
The End

Some people really don't like this self-representation.
Well, I guess it is a fly. It is a bug. (But it looks like me.)
The buglike part of it.

Once I fall in love with someone, I spend all my time thinking about how to make that someone mine. Once I've finally made that someone mine, I spend all my time thinking about how to make that someone happy. I'll still love that someone in five years, ten years, twenty years... I'll love them forever.

CROWN OF LOVE

Vol. 4
Shojo Beat Edition

STORY & ART BY YUN KOUGA

Translation **HC Language Solutions, Inc.**
Touch-up Art & Lettering **Annaliese Christman**
Design **Frances O. Liddell**
Editor **Carrie Shepherd**

VP, Production **Alvin Lu**
VP, Sales & Product Marketing **Gonzalo Ferreyra**
VP, Creative **Linda Espinosa**
Publisher **Hyoe Narita**

Printed in the U.S.A.

Published by VIZ Media, LLC
P.O. Box 77010
San Francisco, CA 94107

10 9 8 7 6 5 4 3 2 1
First printing, November 2010

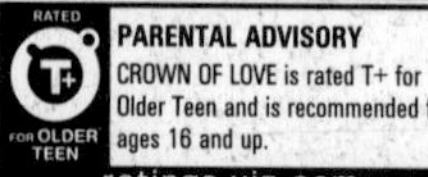

www.viz.com

www.shojobeat.com

Gestalt
BY YUN KOUGA
A CRISIS OF FAITH
A priest in a magical land sets off on a quest to uncover the secrets of a forbidden island. But is the world ready for the demonic truth he'll find?
Find out in the Gestalt manga series—buy yours today!
Gestalt
GESTALT 1 YUN KOUGA
1
STORY & ART BY
YUN KOUGA
From the Creator of Loveless!
On sale at store.viz.com
Also available at your local bookstore or comic store
RATED
T+
FOR OLDER TEEN
ratings.viz.com
VIZ media
www.viz.com
© Yun Kouga / ICHIJINSHA